SCRUFFY

SCRUFFY

By PEGGY PARISH
Pictures by Kelly Oechsli

HarperCollins*Publishers*

This book is a presentation of Newfield Publications, Inc.
Newfield Publications offers book clubs for children
from preschool through high school. For further
information write to: **Newfield Publications, Inc.,**
4343 Equity Drive, Columbus, Ohio 43228.

Published by arrangement with HarperCollins Publishers.
Newfield Publications is a federally registered trademark
of Newfield Publications, Inc. I Can Read Book is a registered
trademark of HarperCollins Publishers.

1995 edition

Scruffy

Library of Congress Cataloging-in-Publication Data
Parish, Peggy.
  Scruffy.

  (An I can read book)
  Summary: Todd chooses a cat from the animal shelter for his
birthday present.
  [1. Cats—Fiction.   2. Birthdays—Fiction]
I. Oechsli, Kelly, ill.   II. Title.   III. Series.
PZ7.P219Sc 1988   [E]   87-45564
ISBN 0-06-024659-6
ISBN 0-06-024660-X (lib. bdg.)

For Scruffy's friends—
Julie and Mack Kennedy
and
Layla and Charlie Wald—
with love

Todd ran into the kitchen.

"Here comes the birthday boy,"

said Dad.

"And here are his birthday pancakes,"

said Mom.

"With my wishing candle!" cried Todd.

Todd closed his eyes.

He made a wish.

Then he blew out the candle.

"I hope it comes true," said Mom.

"So do I," said Todd.

"Are all those presents mine?"

"Every one of them," said Dad.

"Can I open them now?" asked Todd.

"Sure," said Mom.

Todd tore the paper

from a large package.

"Whoopee!" he yelled.

"A scratching post!

My wish is coming true."

Todd quickly opened

the other presents—

a litter pan, litter, cat toys,

cat food, cat dishes.

Then Todd looked all around.

"Where is it?" he asked.

"Where is what?" asked Mom.

"My cat!" said Todd.

"At the animal shelter," said Dad.

"We thought *you* should choose your cat," said Mom.

"Let's go, then," cried Todd.

Dad looked at his watch.

"It's not open yet," he said.

"And you haven't eaten breakfast," said Mom.

"No problem," said Todd.

"I love pancakes."

Soon his plate was clean.

"Can we go *now*?" asked Todd.

"We will go in thirty minutes," said Dad.

"Then I will get things ready
for my cat," said Todd.

He put litter
in the litter pan.

He washed
the cat dishes.

And he watched the clock.

Finally Todd said,

"Please can we go now?

I want to be the first one there."

"All right," said Dad.

The ride seemed to last forever.

"I want a kitten," said Todd.

"Do they have kittens?"

"We will soon find out," said Dad.

Dad parked the car

next to a long building.

"Ten more minutes," Dad said.

"I will wait at the door,"

said Todd.

Todd ran to the door.

He hopped
on one foot.
Then he hopped
on the other.

Finally the door opened.

Todd ran inside.

"Hello," said Todd.

"My name is Todd.

It is my birthday today,

and I came to get a cat."

The woman smiled.

"Good morning, Todd.

I am Mrs. Star.

We have lots of cats.

I am glad you came

to the animal shelter

to choose your pet.

Please follow me."

Todd and his parents

followed Mrs. Star.

A woman came up to them.

"Where are the dogs?" she asked.

"The dogs are in the room

behind the red door,"

said Mrs. Star.

"I didn't know you had dogs,"

said Todd.

"Oh, yes," said Mrs. Star.

"We also have birds, rabbits,

and snakes," said Mrs. Star.

"We even have a monkey."

"Where do you get so many animals?"

asked Todd.

"Some people get tired of their pets,"

said Mrs. Star.

"Or their pets have babies.

When they don't want the babies,

they bring them here."

"I will never get tired of my cat,"

said Todd.

Just then the doorbell rang.

"I will be right back,"

said Mrs. Star.

She opened the door.

A man stood there.

He was holding a box.

"I found these at the dump,"

he said.

"Will you take them?"

"Yes," said Mrs. Star.

"We will make room for them."

The man put down the box.

Todd looked inside.

"Baby puppies!" he cried.

"Why were they at the dump?"

"Somebody threw them away,"

said the man.

"How could they!"

said Todd.

"Can they be punished?"

"If they are caught,"

said Mrs. Star.

"But enough of that, Todd.

Let's go and find you a cat."

Todd and his parents

followed Mrs. Star

into the cat room.

The room was lined
with cages.
The cages were filled
with cats.
There were big cats
and little cats.
There were fat cats
and skinny cats.

30

"How will I know

the right one for me?" asked Todd.

"You will know," said Mrs. Star.

Todd went from cage to cage.

He looked at each cat.

He looked at each kitten.

"Come and see this one," called Mom.

She was holding a fluffy kitten.

"Isn't she pretty?"

"Yes, she is," said Todd.

He scratched the kitten's head.

"Todd," called Dad.

"Look at this handsome fellow."

"He is nice," said Todd.

"But I want to look some more."

Todd looked into the next cage.

Two tiny gray kittens

tumbled over each other.

A black-and-white kitten watched them.

It was older.

Todd liked the gray kittens.

"You are so cute," he said.

Todd wanted to touch them.

He stuck his finger in the cage.

Mrs. Star saw him.

"Would you like to hold one?"

she asked.

"Yes, please," said Todd.

Mrs. Star opened the cage.

Todd took the smallest kitten.

The kitten cried.

Todd stroked it gently.

"Don't be afraid," he said.

"I won't hurt you.

Is it a boy or a girl?" Todd asked.

"That one is a girl," said Mrs. Star.

"The other two are boys."

The older kitten meowed.

"I can't take you now," said Todd.

"My hands are full."

The older kitten walked

to the back of the cage.

He did not look at Todd.

But Todd looked at him.

"Hey, don't be mad," said Todd.

The older kitten stuck up his tail.

Todd laughed and said,

"Your tail is crooked!"

The older kitten twitched his tail.

"I'm sorry," said Todd.

"I should not have laughed at you.

I like your crooked tail."

The kitten still

would not look at Todd.

Todd put the baby kitten

back into the cage.

The older kitten turned around.

But he did not look at Todd.

"Come on," said Todd.

"Let's be friends."

The older kitten turned his back

to Todd again.

"Then be that way," said Todd.

"I will look some more."

Todd saw a girl holding a kitten.

"Mommy," called the girl.

"I found the kitten I want."

"Oh, Janet," said her mother.

"What a cute one.

Is it a male?"

"No," said Mrs. Star.

"It is a female."

"Janet," said her mother,

"we cannot have a female."

"Why not?" asked Janet.

"I really want her."

"Females grow up and have kittens,"
said Janet's mother.

"Does she have to have kittens?"
asked Janet.

"No," said Mrs. Star.

"She can be neutered."

"What is that?" asked Janet.

"It is a simple operation,"

said Mrs. Star.

"Your vet can do it.

Or you can have our vet do it."

"And she will never have kittens?"

asked Janet.

"That is right," said Mrs. Star.

"She will also be healthier."

"In that case," said Janet's mother,

"you may have your kitten, dear."

"Hurrah!" cried Janet.

Todd walked back to the cage
with the three kittens.

The baby kittens were sleeping.
"Meow," cried the older kitten.

Todd laughed and said,

"So you're speaking to me now."

The kitten stuck his paw

out of the cage.

Todd shook it and said,

"I am pleased to meet you."

"Mrs. Star, may I hold him?"

asked Todd.

"Of course," said Mrs. Star.

She gave the kitten to Todd.

"He looks surprised," said Todd.

"He doesn't get held often,"

said Mrs. Star.

"He has been here a month."

"That's a long time," said Todd.

The kitten began to purr.

Todd smiled.

The kitten looked up at Todd.

He purred louder.

And Todd knew!

"Mom! Dad!" he called.

"I have found my kitten."

Mom and Dad looked at the kitten.

They looked at Todd.

"Are you really sure?" asked Dad.

"Yes!" said Todd.

"This is my cat.

His name is Scruffy."

Mom and Dad smiled.

"He *is* sure," said Mom.

"Welcome to the family, Scruffy,"

said Dad.

"Mrs. Star," said Mom.

"Should Scruffy be neutered?"

"Mom!" cried Todd.

"Scruffy is a boy.

He can't be a mother."

"But he can be a father,"

said Mrs. Star.

"Animal shelters are too crowded.

Often we have to put animals to sleep."

Everyone was silent.

Todd cuddled Scruffy closely.

"We will have Scruffy neutered,"

he said.

"Now can we go home?"

"I need a few minutes first,"

said Mrs. Star.

She gave a piece of paper to Todd.

"What is it?" asked Todd.

"It is a promise," said Mrs. Star.

ANIMAL SHELTER

I PROMISE

TO TAKE CARE OF

Scruffy

I WILL GIVE HIM FOOD
AND WATER
·
I WILL KEEP HIM SAFE
·
I WILL GIVE HIM LOVE
·

----------- OWNER

Can you promise all of that?"

"You bet I can," said Todd.

He hugged Scruffy.

"Where do I sign?" he asked.

Dad gave Todd a pen.

"Sign on this line," he said.

Todd carefully wrote his name.

He gave the paper

back to Mrs. Star.

"Now Scruffy is really yours,"

she said.

"I'm glad you chose him."

Todd looked at Scruffy.

Scruffy purred loudly.

"Scruffy needs me," said Todd.

Then he added quietly,

"And I need him."

AAK-5519